Zebedee Zing,
Taster to the King

Damon Burnard

Collins

First published by A & C Black (Publishers) Ltd 1998
Published by Collins in 1998

10 9 8 7 6 5 4 3 2 1

Collins is an imprint of HarperCollins Publishers Ltd,
77/85 Fulham Palace Road, London W6 8JB

Copyright © 1998 Damon Burnard
All rights reserved.

ISBN 0–00–675–356–6

Printed and bound in Great Britain by Caledonian International Book Manufacturing Ltd,
Glasgow G64

Chapter One

Once upon a time, in a land three
bus rides away, there lived a boy
named Zebedee Zing.

Here's Zebedee, doing his most
favourite thing in the whole, wide
world . . .

Children want to be all kinds of
things when they grow up . . .

And Zebedee Zing?

Chapter Two

When Zebedee was old enough to leave school, he didn't go to Clown University, the Royal Academy of Toilet Cleaning, the College of Dentistry, the School for Vets or even the Institute for Mad Scientists in Zurich.

Zebedee became a waiter in a posh restaurant instead!

This restaurant was so posh, even the rats in the kitchen spoke French!

Zebedee loved being a waiter. The trouble was the food smelt so good, he could never resist taking a nibble . . .

But the little nibble would turn into
a BIG BITE . . .

. . . and by the time he reached the
hungry diner, there'd be nothing
left at all!

Zebedee didn't work at the posh
restaurant for very long!

Next, Zebedee got a job delivering pizzas . . .

But the pizzas smelt so good, he could never resist taking a little bite . . .

The little bite would turn into lots of BIG BITES . . .

. . . and by the time he reached his destination, there'd be nothing left at all!

Zebedee didn't deliver pizzas for very long!

Next Zebedee got a job at the
Museum of Natural History.

But looking at dinosaur bones all
day made him very hungry. One
afternoon, Zebedee couldn't resist
taking one teeny-weeny, tincey-
wincey bone to gnaw on . . .

Unfortunately, it turned out to be a very important, teeny-weeny, tincey-wincey bone indeed!

Zebedee didn't work at the Museum of Natural History for very long!

Chapter Three

Before long, there was only one job
left for Zebedee to do. He had to
wear a bright orange suit and a
little orange, triangular hat, and he
had to stand very, very still . . .

Zebedee was a traffic cone on the
motorway!

Sadly for Zebedee, there was
nothing on the motorway to chomp,
or chew, or guzzle – except for the
occasional bug!

What's more, Zebedee only earned
enough money to buy second-hand
eggs and old chickens' livers for his
supper!

Zebedee Zing was a miserable thing!

His one delight was to visit the
Royal Palace, which stood regal and
palatial on the other side of town.

Zebedee would tippy-toe over to the kitchen window and watch while a dozen cooks prepared dazzlingly delightful delicious delicacies . . .

'Trembling truffles!' exclaimed Zebedee.

Chapter Four

In that palace,
lived a king.
This is the
Royal Portrait
of him. ➡️

 In fact, he looked
more like this . . .

Like most kings, the king had big
ears. This was a good thing, as
without them, his crown would
slide down, and he'd end up looking
like this . . .

The king had a
whole room, just
for his toys . . .

He had his
own, private
cinema . . .

He swam in
a pool of
chocolate
milk . . .

. . . and he
had those
twelve cooks
I mentioned
on page 15 . . .

And yet, despite all this, the king was not the Happiest Person Ever. Instead, he was the Most Suspicious.

For a start, he didn't believe people when they were nice to him.

He imagined they said nasty things about him behind his back, and hatched evil plots against him.

'Humph!' he'd think. 'They're
jealous of my palace and my toys
and my pool and my cinema and
my cooks.'

The king was especially worried
about someone stealing his crown
while he slept. And so he spread a
rumour that a ferocious man-eating
lion guarded him at night.

However, like most rumours, this
rumour was not 100% true . . .

The only lion the king really had
was the soft and fuzzy one that sat
upon his pillow.

The king called it Lion, except when
he was sure that no-one was
listening, and then he called it
Liony-Wiony. He'd hold Liony-
Wiony tight through the dark, inky
night, when the shadows came
a-creeping. It made him feel less
afraid.

Chapter Five

Just lately, the king had grown especially suspicious of his cooks. 'What if they slip some sleeping potion into my food?' he thought.

To be on the safe side, the king ate very little of the sumptuous treats that the cooks prepared . . .

He was indeed a skinny kind of king.

As an extra precaution, the king would tippy-toe out of the back door and spy on the cooks through the kitchen window.

But one day, to his surprise . . .

. . . someone was there ahead of him!

Chapter Six

'YOU THERE!' said the king, in the bravest voice he could muster.

'No,' said Zebedee. 'I'm not!'

'Because if you *are* plotting against me, I'll have to set my lion on you,' said the king.

But Zebedee wasn't listening. He was too busy staring into the kitchen, his eyes as wide as saucers. 'Galloping gorgonzola!' he gushed.

Suddenly the king had an idea.

'What would I have to do, exactly?'
asked Zebedee.
The king explained that his job
would be to taste the king's food
before he did, to make sure it was
safe to eat.

'That way,' added the king, 'I wouldn't have to spy on the cooks any more . . .'

'I'll do it!' yelled Zebedee, leaping joyously into the air.

But the job wasn't his. Not yet.

Not only was the king:

a) skinny, and
b) suspicious, he was also
c) cautious, and
d) officious.

And so, before making Zebedee his Official Taster, the king gave him a Royal Taster's Test.

Zebedee never thought that a test could be so much fun!

Here's Zebedee's report card; as you can see, he did well on everything . . . well, nearly everything!

Effort 10
Enthusiasm 10
Zeal 10
Ardour 10
Vigour 10
Fervour 10
Thoroughness 10
Speed 10
Energy 10
Table Manners 0
                          90
TOTAL 100

And so, in a single day, Zebedee went from being a chicken-liver chomping, second-hand egg eating, bug-crunching traffic cone, to Zebedee Zing, Taster to the King!

Chapter Seven

Here's Zebedee in his Royal
Taster's Uniform . . .

Zebedee loved his new job. Being a
traffic cone had been very lonely –
especially in the rain and the cold.
But now he could spend the day
strolling through the king's lovely,
warm palace.

He also liked spending time with the king, even if he was moody and grouchy, and didn't know how to share . . .

But most of all, Zebedee loved tasting the cooks' fabulous food; their chips, for example, were perfect!

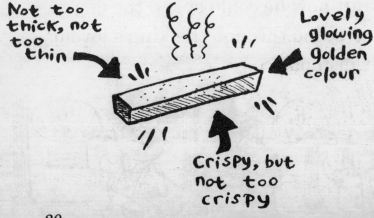

At first the king was very pleased with himself, for in Zebedee he had found the World's Greatest Taster.

The trouble was, Zebedee was so Great, there was never much left for the king to taste!

The king became so very skinny,
when he stood sideways, he was
nearly invisible.

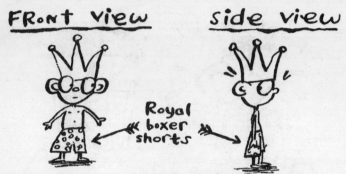

FRoNT VIEW   side view

Royal boxer shorts

Each night he went to bed a little
hungrier, and his tummy growled a
little louder than the night before.

'Oh well!' grumbled the king.

It's a small price to pay, to know that my crown is safe!

Grrr!

But deep down, he wasn't so sure . . .

Chapter Eight

As the days went by, the king got hungrier and hungrier. By the time his birthday came around, he was too hungry to remember which one it was. He'd just narrowed it down to either his ninth, or his forty-second, when the Head Chef burst in.

'In honour of this glorious occasion,' the Head Chef cheerfully announced, 'we have prepared a birthday surprise!' And with that, he clicked his fingers. Twice.

In came the cooks, carrying a huge
gift-wrapped THING.

'Uh-oh chungo!' thought the king.
'What can it be?'

With trembling fingers he undid the
bow, to reveal . . .

'That's right, Your Royal
Skinnyness!' said the Head Chef.
'A cake! And on top we've written
"We love you" in chocolate chips!'

The king's heart melted like a scoop of ice cream on a dragon's tongue. 'Oh thank you!' he cried.

Not only did the king forget about being suspicious, he couldn't even remember why he had been in the first place! He was so pleased he gave everyone the day off, then away he ran to fetch a spoon. Oh, and a ladder.

Just as the king was about to dive
into the cake, in rushed Zebedee.
'WAIT!' he screamed.

For once, the king wasn't sure.

'No, I don't think so,' he said.

'What, absolutely sure?' asked
Zebedee.

'Maybe Zebedee is right!' thought
the king. 'After all, something bad
is bound to happen to me on my
birthday!'

He climbed down the ladder and
weighed up the pros and cons, the
fors and againsts and the pluses
and minuses.

At last he decided that Zebedee
should taste it.

'I promise!' promised Zebedee.
'Now, please get out of my way!' he
cried, and he jumped into the cake,
head first.

Chapter Nine

'Well?' asked the king, after a while.

'I need a few more mouthfuls!' said Zebedee.

A little later, the king asked him again.

And so it went on, and on, until there was just one crumb left.

'Oh no!' thought the king.

'MY CAKE!'

He made a dash for the crumb . . .

desperate leap!

But Zebedee got there first!

In desperation the king watched as
Zebedee flicked the crumb into his
mouth.

'DELICIOUS!' he exclaimed. And
then he noticed the king, lying on
the empty plate.

'Oh, hello!' he said.

Chapter Ten

Normally the king was a quiet kind of king, and even when he was cross he'd just smoulder and fume like a damp rag over a dull flame.

But at that moment he was Extra-specially Super Cross!

He went all red in the face and
bounced about, up and down and all
around, shouting all the while . . .

Zebedee felt terrible. He was filled
with remorse (see diagram).

Diagram:
Zebedee
filled
with
remorse

level
of
remorse

NB: shaded area
represents remorse.

'I'm sorry, King!' he cried.

And with that he snatched the hat
from Zebedee's head – the hat
Zebedee loved so much – and
jumped on it.

Jumping on it once would've been
bad enough, but the king jumped on
it over and over again, until
Zebedee couldn't bear to watch.

'GET OUT!' shouted the king.

Zebedee Zing made for the door, for
he was Taster to the King no more!

Chapter Eleven

'Typical!' grumbled the king.

He was so hungry and cross, he decided that there was nothing left to do but wait until bed-time.

Now his palace was empty, it was an awfully long and quiet wait – especially without Zebedee bounding and crashing about!

At last the clock struck bed-time, and the king crabbily climbed the stairs. 'I bet someone tries to steal my crown tonight!' he thought.

And you know what? He was right!

That dark and inky night, just as he was dropping off to sleep, a burglar stole through his window . . .

'Hello, King!' said the burglar.

'Oh, h-hello!' said the king.

'Oh,' said the king.

'No,' said the burglar, again.

'Oh,' said the king. 'I thought as much!'

And then the burglar saw Liony-Wiony.

'Ha ha!' he sniggered.

'I've a real lion too!' said the king, trying not to sound nervous, which was difficult, because he was very nervous indeed.

'And he'll p-pounce at any moment!'

The burglar roared with laughter. He snatched up Liony-Wiony and pranced around the room, chanting in a singy-songy voice.

'Ha! Ha! Ha!' he mocked, when he'd finished. 'What a silly king you are!' But as he reached out to grab the king's crown . . .

. . . there was a loud . . .

"ROAR!"

'Eeek!' squealed the burglar.

Then . . .

"ROAR!"

The burglar turned as white as a
sheet and trembled like a plate of
jelly rollerblading down a
cobblestone street.

"ROAR!"

"IT'S A LION!"

'I'm getting out of here!' screamed
the burglar. He turned on his heels
and leapt out of the window.

ARRGHH!

Bdoing!

Chapter Twelve

SO...

Did the king have a fierce, man-eating lion after all?

NO!

It was the rowdy rumblings of a royal tummy that the robber mistook for a ravenous roar! Really!

How felicitous!

said the king, which is a fancy way of saying that the whole thing was very lucky indeed.

'Thank goodness for Zebedee Zing!' he thought.

The king jumped out of bed and
raced over to Zebedee's house in his
pyjamas.

He found the Ex-taster to the king
sitting in a corner, looking very
sorry for himself.

He was indeed a sorrowful sight!

To Zebedee's surprise the king strode over and gave him a big hug . . .

. . . and a hearty slap on the back.

'Thank goodness for Zebedee Zing, the World's Greatest Taster!' said the king, and he told Zebedee all about the burglar.

When he'd finished, the king asked
Zebedee to come back to the palace.
'I'd love to!' said Zebedee, because
he'd missed the king and the palace
very much indeed.

'That's true!' said the king.

Chapter Thirteen

Here's Zebedee in his new
uniform . . .

And here's the king in his new
crown (actually it's the same crown
– he just wrote on it, that's all!)

Together they played . . .

. . . and watched movies . . .

. . . and splashed around in
chocolate milk!

And when it came to dinner time,
Zebedee ate a little less, and the
king ate a little more, more or
less . . .

And the burglar? He was found the
very next day, and made to wash up
all the big, greasy pans in the
twelve cooks' kitchen, until he was
really, truly sorry . . .

And so Zebedee Zing and the king
lived happily ever after . . .

. . . except, perhaps, for when it was time for dessert!